"Sylva, I won't tell you again. You are not to go near a Summer Cottage or a Summer Dog or a Summer Cat or any of the Summer People. It is simply too dangerous. Do you understand?"

Sylva's eyes welled up.

"Sylva understands now," said Rosy gently to Clara. She hated to see Sylva so upset. "Don't you, Sylva?"

"I guess so."

"Good," said Rosy. "Then we'll all be safe."

It did not occur to Rosy then, or for a long time afterward, that it might be she who would trespass into the world of the Summer People.

THE fairy bell SISTERS

Rosy
and the
Secret Friend

Margaret McNamara

ILLUSTRATIONS BY JULIA DENOS

BALZER + BRAY
An Imprint of HarperCollinsPublishers

In the spirit of J. M. Barrie, who created Peter Pan and Tinker Bell, the author has donated a portion of the proceeds from the sale of this book to the Great Ormond Street Hospital.

Balzer + Bray is an imprint of HarperCollins Publishers.

Rosy and the Secret Friend
Text copyright © 2013 by Margaret McNamara
Illustrations copyright © 2013 by Julia Denos

Library of Congress Cataloging-in-Publication Data
McNamara, Margaret.
Rosy and the secret friend / Margaret McNamara ; illustrations by Julia Denos. — 1st ed.
p. cm. — (The fairy Bell sisters)
Summary: "Usually, when the Summer People take over the cottages of Sheepskerry Island, the Fairy Bell Sisters go into hiding, but when kind-hearted Rosy realizes that a Summer Child named Louisa needs help, she does the unthinkable and befriends her"— provided by publisher.
ISBN 978-0-06-222805-5 (hardcover bdg. : alk. paper)
ISBN 978-0-06-222804-8 (pbk. bdg. : alk. paper)
[1. Fairies—Fiction. 2. Sisters—Fiction. 3. Friendship—Fiction. 4. Secrets—Fiction.] I. Denos, Julia, ill. II. Title.
PZ7.M47879343Ros 2013   2012038106
[Fic]—dc23   CIP
                                                                                  AC

Typography by Erin Fitzsimmons
14 15 16 17 CG/OPM 10 9 8 7 6 5 4
❖
First Edition

for
Laura & Louisa

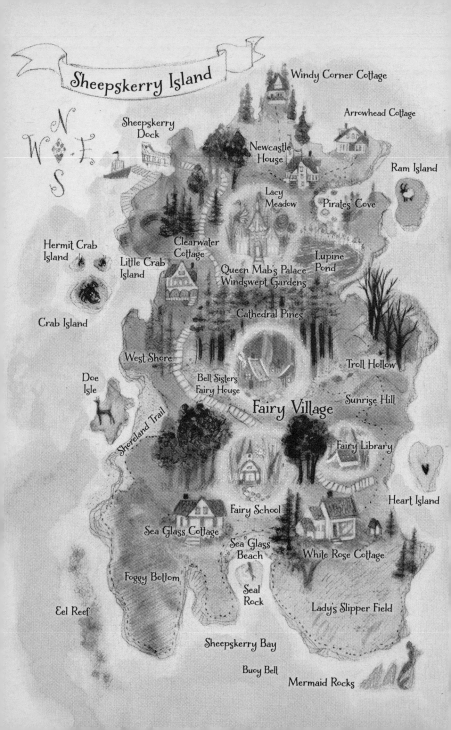

THE
fairy bell
SISTERS

one

All the fairies in the wide world love summer—except the Fairy Bell sisters and their friends on Sheepskerry Island. Sheepskerry is a fairies' paradise in fall and winter and spring, and summer should be the best season of all. And for a while, it is.

In June, fairies start doing the things they've been meaning to do all the rest of the year: The Stitch sisters sew costumes for dress-up games; the Cobwebs crochet delicate fairy shawls; the Flower sisters take out their watercolors and paint under the pale-blue sky.

In July it's time to throw off fairy wings and

jump in Lupine Pond and splash in the cool water. Then there are berries for the picking, all over the island—pinkberries first, and most delicate; then raspberries, blueberries, mulberries, boysenberries, and finally blackberries when the days are hottest. The Bakewell sisters make pies and muffins with the freshest of the pick, and the older Jellicoe sisters swiftly put up jams and jellies for the winter months if the berry bushes are especially bountiful.

When at the end of the day the fireflies light up and the summer sun goes down, the fairies are ready to lay their heads on thistledown pillows and dream fairy dreams. But first they watch the sunset on the West Shore, which every night paints the sky lavender, purple, gold, and scarlet, and needs no fairy magic to be beautiful.

Summer on Sheepskerry Island would be perfect, except for the month of August. In August, the Summer People come.

Summer People are just that. They're people. Human beings. Mothers and fathers. Girls and boys. Most of them mean well, of course, but still they are immense, bumbling creatures who trample fairy gardens and unleash barking dogs and circle the island in stinky boats and altogether turn a fairy paradise into a dreadful place. So fairies stay in their houses under the Cathedral Pines and only come out safely at night. The Fairy Bell sisters love the summer weather and the fruits and flowers of the garden. They love the long days and the cool nights. But they don't love hiding from the Summer People. Yet hide they must.

two

Don't tell me you are one of the very few children who have not met the Fairy Bell sisters! You are in for a treat, for you can meet them now. Allow me to introduce you to:

Clara Bell   Rosy Bell

Golden Bell   Sylva Bell

and baby Squeak

(They are Tinker Bell's little sisters, by the way.)

If you are anything like me, you'd never

suspect that one of the Fairy Bell sisters would end up keeping a secret from her sisters—a very big secret indeed. But just last summer, Rosy Bell did something that she hoped her sisters would never find out. It was an act of kindness, of course, an act of very great and courageous kindness, but it led Rosy into trouble and the fairies of Sheepskerry Island into danger—perhaps the gravest danger those fairies had ever known.

I'd better get this said right now: If your idea of a good book is one where everyone does everything right all the time, then you're not going to enjoy this one very much.

If, though, you can bear to read about Rosy's kindness to a little sick girl, and how it made her sisters ashamed of her—even though they knew Rosy had done the right thing—then take a deep breath and turn the page.

three

Yᴏᴜ turned the page!
What a good choice you've made!

four

"It's the Summer People!"

Rosy heard Sylva Bell's cry, and her heart sank. She tried not to think bad thoughts about anyone in the world, but even Rosy could not think too kindly about the Summer People.

"Now we'll have to stay in the house all day, as they unpack and unload." Goldie sighed deeply. "What a bore."

"We could play Go Fish in the Fairy Pond," said Rosy, "just to pass the time." Go Fish in the Fairy Pond is very much like our card game called Go Fish, but there are no kings or jacks in the deck, and the jokers are trolls. Rosy started to deal.

Last year's crop of Summer People had not discovered the fairies' lovely houses, for their eyes did not know how to see magic, and their ears could not hear the music of fairy voices, and that was a blessing.

"How long has our house stood here, Clara?" Sylva asked. "Goldie, do you have any...sevens?"

"A very long time, Sylva, longer than anyone can remember. Houses are terribly hard to build, as young fairy magic does not extend to architecture."

"Architecture?" asked Sylva.

"House building," said Goldie. "No sevens. Go fish in the fairy pond."

"In fact," Clara continued, "a long time ago, before any of us popped into the world, the fairies of Sheepskerry Island lived in abandoned birds' nests."

"Birds' nests!" said Sylva.

"I suppose it might not have been too bad," said Rosy.

"I could not possibly have lived in a bird's nest," said Goldie. "Far too scratchy for my delicate skin."

"In those days, Summer People were quite lovely," Clara went on. "There were only a few of them, and they lived very simply. They built the six cottages that are on Sheepskerry now: Newcastle, Arrowhead, Clearwater, Windy Corner, Sea Glass, and White Rose Cottage."

"White Rose Cottage is my favorite," said Rosy with a sigh.

"Of course, the cottages have gotten much bigger and fancier now—" said Clara.

"Except for White Rose—" said Rosy.

"Because the Summer People have changed. The grown-ups, at least."

"Clara, do you have any queens?" asked Goldie. She looked out the window of the great room. "Do you suppose Queen Mab is enjoying her holiday?"

"I'm sure she is," said Clara. "No queens."

"It is funny not to have her here," said Sylva, touching the necklace Queen Mab had given her after the Fairy Ball not long ago. "Maybe I could fly over to Heart Island sometime and just drop in."

"I don't think so," said Goldie, as she rearranged her cards.

"Please, can we get back to the story now?" asked Rosy.

Clara started again. "Back in those days," she said, "children looked for fairies every morning when the dew was still fresh on the spiders' webs. Summer Children and fairies played together. Of course, the fairies did not really show themselves—or not too much, anyway— but they left little gifts for the Summer Children, and the Summer Children left gifts for them."

Rosy looked over at the fireplace mantel in their great room. There was a tiny seashell, painted bright pink.

"That was a gift from a long-ago Summer Child," said Rosy. "She gave it to Tinker Bell, or at least that's how the story goes." No one was quite sure whether that was true, but they liked to believe it was.

"The Summer Children's greatest gift was the Fairy Village in Cathedral Pines," said Clara.

"Pah-pah!" said Squeak.

"Yes, Squeakie. It *is* rather amazing. Summer Children built our fairy houses, one for every family of fairy sisters who live on Sheepskerry. And it's those houses we live in to this very day."

The sisters paused to think about those long-ago days. Their thoughts were interrupted by a clattering din coming from the dock, where the Summer People were arriving on the ferry.

Goldie peered out the window. "Now the Summer People are horrible," she said. "They're especially horrible on Moving-In Day. We'll be trapped in this hot house till nightfall because of them."

"I'm sure they don't mean to be so thoughtless," said Rosy.

"I'm sure they do," said Goldie. "They spoil everything, every year." And she put her cards down. "It's no use," she said. "I can't concentrate with all this noise. Let's hide up in Tall Birch and watch them."

The Summer People were unloading the ferry and carrying all their many possessions up the boardwalks to the cottages. It took a long time, as Sheepskerry Island had no roads and no horrible metal monsters ("They're called 'automobiles,'" said Clara), and the Summer People filled up wheelbarrows to bring their boxes and bags, trunks and trinkets, to the cottages on the island. Sylva flew up to a lookout post. "Looks like there are five families this year, so one cottage will be empty," she called down to her sisters. "That's a relief."

"Wuh!" said Squeak.

"Yes, I'd love to do something about it, Squeakie," said Rosy. "But there's nothing we

can do. We must just put up with them as best we can. Five families is an awful lot." She sighed. "But I suppose it's better than six. Be careful up there, Sylva!"

"I wonder why they need to bring so much stuff."

"And why must they make such a racket?" asked Goldie. "Don't they know how sensitive we are?"

"Come down at once, Sylva," called Clara. "You mustn't be seen."

"Just one more minute—"

"Now, Sylva," said Rosy.

Sylva flew down from the birch as her sister told her. "I wouldn't mind flying into a cottage while they're in there, just to see what the cottages are like when the Summer People are inside them," she said. "I could sneak up on—"

"Oh dear me, no," said Rosy, as crossly as she knew how (which wasn't very crossly at all).

"You mustn't do anything like that. The Summer People are to be kept away from at all costs."

"Rosy's quite right," said Golden. "If these human people were to see our magic and discover that fairies live here, they'd tell all their friends, who'd come hunt for us with those telescope things—"

"Cameras."

"Yes, with cameras and torches and rakes and goodness knows what else. And that will be the end of us."

"But if we—"

"Hush, Sylva, that's enough," said Clara in a clipped tone. "You remember what happened on Coombe Meadow Island, don't you?" Clara didn't like to have to bring up faraway Coombe Meadow, but she had to stop Sylva's wild ideas.

The other sisters, even Squeak, fell silent. "Did all the fairies lose their homes?" asked Sylva at last.

"Every one of them. Their houses were trampled, their school was dug up, their queen's palace was destroyed—" Rosy had to stop for breath.

"—and many of them were chased till they dropped from exhaustion. So it is lucky that they all escaped." Clara didn't add "with their lives." She didn't need to.

"I thought Summer People were nice to fairies," said Sylva.

"Oh, they used to be nice to fairies," said Clara. "When children still believed in fairies." She sighed. "But those children don't exist anymore."

(How I wish Clara knew about you!)

"So if we value our homes and our lives and Sheepskerry Island, we must stay far away."

"Still, if I was very careful—"

"Sylva, I won't tell you again. You are not to go near a Summer Cottage or a Summer Dog or a Summer Cat or any of the Summer People. It is simply too dangerous. Do you understand?"

Sylva's eyes welled up.

"Sylva understands now," said Rosy gently to Clara. She hated to see Sylva so upset. "Don't you, Sylva?"

"I guess so."

"Good," said Rosy. "Then we'll all be safe."

It did not occur to Rosy then, or for a long time afterward, that it might be she who would trespass into the world of the Summer People.

five

By the end of the day, the five families had moved into their summer cottages. Peace came over the island at last.

The sisters missed the fireflies that evening, and the sunset, but when they peeked their heads out of their fairy house and saw a roof of bright stars in the heavens, the waste of the day did not feel so bad.

"We only have a little time before we need to go to bed," said Clara. "Let's see what damage the Summer People have done so far. That way, we'll know the worst of it before we start setting things to rights in the morning."

Rosy fetched a lantern and put in a tiny bit of jellyfish phosphorescence, which lit up the bright night even more. Sylva took Squeak in her arms, and off they all went to explore.

"Dhaah," said Squeak.

"Yes, it is dark, Squeak, but you're safe," said Goldie.

They traced the Summer People's path from cottage to cottage and found, as they'd expected, that the Summer People had been as careless as ever.

The shell-lined path up to the Blossom sisters' house was at sixes and sevens, and the dogs had been up to mischief in the gardens near the Seashell sisters' place. "I'll have to replant those mulberry bushes," said Clara with a sigh. "More work, just when I thought I'd get a rest."

In front of Deepwater Spring, where they washed and dried the laundry, Rosy's face fell. "Oh dear," she said. "Here's a week's worth

of washing, trampled underfoot." Every one of Squeakie's diapers for the week had been squashed into the mud.

"Odeo!" cried Squeak.

"Never mind, Squeak," said Rosy. "I'll make sure you have fresh ones to keep you dry. But what a lot of work it will be."

A sudden shriek came from Goldie, who was

down on Sea Glass Beach.

"My blues! They're gone!"

Goldie had been collecting bits of blue sea glass ever since fairy school let out. Blue sea glass is the rarest of all, as you probably know, and it's very hard to spot. Goldie happened to have a talent for finding blue sea glass ("Probably because it's the same color as my eyes," she once said), and she had amassed quite a pile of it.

"Poor Goldie!" said Rosy.

"I did mention you should have brought it home to take care of it properly," said Clara.

Goldie had left the blue sea glass in a tiny little tide pool on the beach outside White Rose Cottage so all the other fairies could stop by and admire her treasure.

"How could those Summer People ever have found it so quickly? On the first day! Why, if I ever meet one of those Summer People, I will—"

"Quiet!"

Sylva's voice was urgent.

Then they all heard it. The rumble of a wheel-barrow up the path. People's voices—Summer People's voices. They were headed to White Rose Cottage, just yards from where the Fairy Bell sisters were hovering.

"Squeak!" said Squeak.

"Shhh," said the other sisters together.

Usually the Summer People were happy to come to Sheepskerry Island. The fairies could hear it in their voices and see it in their step. It was the one nice thing about their arrival.

"What's wrong with them?" asked Sylva.

"I don't know," said Rosy.

Their footsteps were heavy, and their voices had a sad note, like the sound of a buoy bell in Sheepskerry Bay. And there was something else, another sound that was unfamiliar to the Bell sisters.

Rosy lifted up her lantern, very, very carefully, so that it would look like no more than the moonlight glinting off a bleached shell. What she saw startled her.

Two big Summer People, a mother and a father, were pushing a cart up the hill to White Rose Cottage. It wasn't a usual cart, crammed with tennis racquets, suitcases, and grocery bags full of food. In fact, it wasn't a cart at all. It was a chair—a chair on wheels. And in it sat a little girl.

"Almost there, Louisa," said the Summer Mother. "Back to White Rose Cottage."

So the sixth cottage would *have a family in it this August*, Rosy thought.

"You love it here," said the Summer Father.

"I don't love it this year," said the girl called Louisa. "I've wrecked everyone's summer already."

"That's not true!" said her mother.

"It is true! You told me I shouldn't jump off that fifth step and I did it anyway, and now my foot is smashed and everybody's summer is spoiled because of me."

"Oh, sweetheart, don't think that way."

Louisa said no more as her father maneuvered the wheeled chair up the steps to the cottage. It took him some time.

It was only because Rosy was so close to the boardwalk path that she heard what Louisa's mother whispered to her husband. "I hope the island will work its magic, Will. It's the only thing that will make her better."

Six

The first week of August for the Bell sisters was not so very bad. They busied themselves during the day, playing together and spending lots of time with Squeak under the cover of Cathedral Pines. Since all the fairies were there together, it was rather like what we would call sleepaway camp. Activities all day, quiet time for telling stories, and singing in the Fairy Circle at night.

The Bell girls were very good singers. "The best," Goldie liked to say. Their voices were as clear and pretty as their names. Possibly their harmonies lacked a little depth after Tink flew off to Neverland, but the four older sisters had learned to make up for Tink's absence with new songs they learned from the mermaids, who had learned them from sailors, who had learned them from children long ago.

There was a strong wind that early August evening, and the Blossom sisters asked for a song to calm the spirits of the Sheepskerry fairies.

"The fairies will rest better if you sing them to sleep," said Apple Blossom.

So, without any more prompting, the Fairy Bell sisters sang an old song:

Oh I know a place where the sun is like gold,
And the cherry blooms burst with snow . . .

"Sheepskerry Island!" cried Julia Jellicoe.

And there on the isle is the loveliest nook,
Where fairies and friendship do grow.

When the Fairy Bell sisters had finished all four verses, the fairies fluttered their wings, which is how fairies clap. Clara gave a small nod, Golden made a deep curtsy, Sylva grinned, and Rosy fluttered her wings toward the other fairies as Squeak (who was already asleep) gave a little

baby-fairy snore. "You're very kind," Rosy said.

"Now quick to bed," said Clara. "And let's hope the wind, when it comes, does not do too much harm to these old trees."

"Or to our fairy houses, either," said Rosy.

Seven

The wind died down, and the fairies slept well that night and the next. A few days later the sun shone as hot and bright as ever on a summer morning. It was a perfect day for a cool swim, and the fairies were certain the Summer Children would head down to the dock and allow them the privacy of a dip in Lupine Pond.

The Summer Children obliged.

Have you ever jumped off a pier into a cold, cold salt bay? It's nothing like jumping into a swimming pool, even a cold one. It's not like a lake or a pond, either, where the sun warms the water.

"I have to admire the Summer People," said Sylva that morning. "The children are fearless when it comes to jumping off the dock. And it's such a long drop when the tide is low!" The sisters were in their fairy house, waiting for the children to do what they always did on days like this and head to the dock.

"Once they're all down on the dock, we can have the freedom of the island," said Goldie.

"A cool dip in Lupine Pond will be just the thing," said Rosy. "Have we all got our bathers?"

"I'd like to go see the Summer Children splash into that water, just once," Sylva said. "I think if I—"

"Sylva, honestly," said Clara.

"All right, then, I'll just listen to them having fun and imagine what it looks like. I bet I can jump higher than they can anyway."

"Good girl," said Rosy.

The boardwalk path down to the dock passed very near the Fairy Bell sisters' house. Suddenly there was a stampede of footsteps.

"They sound like a pack of trolls," said Goldie, with a sniff.

"Are you sure the trolls are all gone?" asked Sylva. Sylva was not very fond of the trolls, as she had once had to do battle with them.

"The trolls piled into their war ship and paddled over to Ram Island, as they do every August," said Clara.

"To fight the seagulls!" cried Goldie, with a merry voice.

"Do they win?" asked Sylva.

"Look up in the sky," said Clara. Looking out the window, she pointed to the seagulls wheeling overhead. "Do the trolls ever win their fights, gulls?" she asked.

The seagulls laughed.

"The trolls shake their fists and toss their

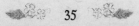

pebbles, but the seagulls pay them no heed," said Clara.

"Then the trolls come back with 'battle stories,'" Rosy told Sylva, "when all they've done is ruffle a few feathers."

All at once, a blur of children passed by the Bell sisters' house.

"Look! There go the boys from Newcastle House—haven't they grown!"

Three more children came pounding down the path. "Those are the Arrowhead children—"

Then came a flurry of arms and legs and wheelbarrows and life jackets. And two panting brown dogs.

"That's all seven cousins from Windy Corner," said Sylva. "They might need me to—"

"And those are the kids from Sea Glass Cottage," said Goldie. "I bet they're the ones who stole my blues."

"Where are the Clearwater kids?" asked Sylva.

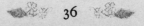

"Lay-lay-lay," said Squeak.

"They're coming, you're right!" said Clara. "Good girl, Squeakie."

And finally the Clearwater Cottage twins trundled down the path, with their big sister in tow.

"That's all of them, isn't it?" asked Clara.

Rosy said nothing.

"Yes, that's it!" said Goldie. "We have our dear island to ourselves!"

"I'm going to find Poppy!" said Sylva. "I haven't seen her in ages."

"If by 'ages' you mean one day," said Goldie. But Sylva didn't hear her. She was already out the door to visit her best friend.

"I'll take Squeak out for an airing," said Clara. And she strapped Squeakie into her fairy stroller.

"Hmm!" said Squeak.

"The beach?" said Clara. "All right, Squeakie. That's where we'll go. Then we can meet up with everyone at the pond later. You coming, Goldie?"

"I suppose so," said Goldie with a sigh. "I'll have to start up my collection again sometime."

"Coming, Rosy?" asked Clara.

"I think I'll stay here and read for a while," said Rosy, a little quieter than usual, though no one much noticed. "It will be nice to have the place all to myself."

"Don't spend the whole day indoors," said Clara. "Stop squirming, Squeak!"

"Let's go," said Goldie. And off they went.

I have no doubt that you've guessed the reason Rosy stayed at home that hot August morning. You've counted the children and you've counted the cottages and you've realized they do not add up to every island cottage and every island child. Let's do it together, just to make sure:

COTTAGES	CHILDREN
Newcastle House	2 boys (much bigger than last year)
Arrowhead Cottage	1 boy, 2 girls
Windy Corner Cottage	7 cousins (no one is sure who's a boy and who's a girl, as they all blend together)

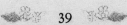

COTTAGES	CHILDREN
Sea Glass Cottage	1 boy, 1 girl
Clearwater Cottage	2 girls (twins)
	1 girl (their older sister)

Rosy did her sums, too. She added up the cottages. "Five. That's one cottage missing," said Rosy to herself. "White Rose Cottage."

Then she added up the children, and her tally told her what she already knew. "That's seventeen children." She heard the squeals of triumphant laughter from the dock. "And there are eighteen children on the island this year. So one child is missing. Louisa."

Rosy went over to the hat rack and tied a fairy sun hat firmly on her head. She left her book unread, pulled open the door to the fairy house, and flew away.

eight

You'd think that White Rose Cottage would be covered with white roses (at least that's what I thought when I first heard about it), but in fact the cottage itself is white, and the roses are every color.

The yellow roses are the first you see, climbing up a trellis on the clapboards in the front of the house. On the shutters, deep orange roses bloom against the dark-green slats. Coral blossoms run along the path to the front door, and bouquets of creamy tea roses line every window box. And the hedge around the cottage is pure pink primrose, fragrant and lovely.

White Rose Cottage

It took Rosy quite a while to fly to White Rose Cottage, as the wind was against her the whole way. When at last she arrived, she flew up the flagstone path. She knew she should not be so close to a cottage, especially as she was fairly certain that there were Summer People inside—or at least one Summer Person.

Rosy kept near the rosebushes as she

approached the beveled windows. *I could be mistaken for a bee*, she thought, though she did not really believe it. She flew quietly to the second floor to peek in the windows. No one in the polka-dot room. No one under the eaves . . .

Suddenly she heard voices along the path.

"I mustn't be spotted!" she cried.

A mother blue jay heard her panicked voice and, seeing that it was Rosy, swooped her up and placed her gently in her own fledglings' nest. Rosy remembered the jay and recalled the time the bright blue bird's clawed foot had caught on a wire. It had taken Rosy a full quarter of an hour to free her that rainy March day.

The jay motioned for Rosy to crouch down. She covered Rosy with a wide-spread wing just as the twins from Clearwater Cottage bounded up the porch to Louisa's house. "Louisa!" they cried. "Lulu! It's us!" Their big sister wasn't far behind.

"Pipe down, Isadora," she said. "You too, Jamie. Louisa might be asleep. We should be quiet."

Rosy watched from the safety of the jay's nest. The screen door to White Rose Cottage swung out slightly. Rosy could just see Louisa's crutch propping it open.

"Lulu! We're going to have a race!" said Isadora. She was hopping up and down on the porch, swamped by her enormous life jacket. "It was Katie's idea." She gave her big sister's legs a hug.

Louisa opened the door a little more. It took quite an effort. "I broke my foot, or didn't you know?" she said. If the twins heard the sorrowful note in her voice, they did not show it.

"We know! We know!" said Jamie. "That's why it's such a great idea."

"We'll run as fast as we can—"

"—and Katie will push you in a wheelbarrow!"

The twins
could not stay
still.

"We'll race
you down to
the dock!"

"It will be funner
than anything!"

Katie spoke gently. "We thought you'd want
to be down with the other kids, Louisa," she
said. "We miss you."

"Go on, Louisa," said Rosy to Louisa in a
whisper. "You can do it."

Louisa hesitated a moment. Then she let the
screen door slam shut.

"I can't come with you," she said.

The mother jay squawked.

"Please come," said Katie.

"Why won't she go?" whispered Rosy.

"Can't you see I'm no good for anything?"

asked Louisa. "I'll just mess it up for every-one else." And she clomped back inside on her crutches, catching herself on the rug in the hall.

The twins stopped their bouncing. Their teeth started to chatter.

"Come on, girlicues," said their sister quietly. "It's getting cold. Let's go home and get some lunch. Race you to the cottage!"

And with that they ran up the boardwalk, though Rosy noticed they were a little slower than before.

Rosy could scarcely believe what she had just witnessed. "If Louisa had looked at the faces on those little girls, she would have had to change her mind," she said to the mother jay.

The jay cocked her head.

"You believe Louisa is only thinking of her-self," said Rosy. "I suppose that's true. But I believe she's thinking the wrong things." Rosy thanked the mother jay; then slowly, carefully, she flew down to the cottage. She was fairly certain now which window would be Louisa's: the downstairs bedroom, where a little girl on crutches would not have to climb any stairs.

Rosy peered in through the window.

And she was shocked at what she saw.

Instead of the cheery guest room she remembered from wintertime visits, there was a dreadful mess of a place. Clothing was strewn all over the floor. The bed was unmade, and the sheets were in a tangle. A jigsaw puzzle was half-abandoned, with most of the pieces facedown. A rather nice painting had been left unfinished. Knitting needles were poking out of a handbag, a cross-stitch sampler was squashed under a stuffed unicorn, playing cards were scattered all over the rag rug, potholder loops were knotted on top of a pile of pick-up sticks, and the big, clear French doors that opened out to a view of Sheepskerry Bay were shuttered tight.

"What a squirrel's nest!" said Rosy. The bees, busy in the window box next to her, hummed agreement. "Who would want to spend a summer in a room like this?"

And then she heard someone crying, crying very hard.

nine

In a corner of the darkened room she saw Louisa. "Why am I so mean?" she sobbed. "It's just a broken foot!"

"A broken foot!" said Rosy to the bees. "That's as bad as a broken wing!"

"Ummm-hmmm," droned the bees.

Louisa tossed her crutches on the floor and balanced precariously on one leg.

"Other kids wouldn't mind a bit," she said between gulps. "Why do I have to be so horrible?" Her shoulders heaved with sobs.

Rosy's kind heart went out to poor Louisa. "I'm sure she's just sad," she said, "not horrible at all. I wish there were someone who could help—"

"Louisa!" called a woman's voice. "Are you okay, honey? I can give you a hand once I'm done with the—"

"No, Mom!" Louisa said. "I don't need any help!"

And with that she threw herself down on the bed and buried her face in the pillow.

"I hate this stupid foot! I hate this stupid island!" And she cried even harder.

The bees hummed for a while, as Rosy watched Louisa and wished she could do her some small kindness. After a while, Louisa's shoulders stilled, and the sobbing stopped.

"I really do wish she'd let someone help her," said Rosy.

"Umm-mmmmmm."

"No one would have to know if I were the one," said Rosy. "She's fast asleep. She won't see me."

"Unh-unhhhh," the bees hummed, a little more loudly.

Just then, Louisa turned over in bed. Her cast knocked a glass of water onto her sketch pad, and her pretty painting turned into a runny mess of colors.

"That's it," said Rosy. "I'll just pop in quickly and make her room feel a bit nicer. Then maybe she'll feel nicer, too."

"Nnnnnnnn-nnnnnnnn," the bees chorused.

"Her mother did say that the island needed to work its magic."

When she thought the bees weren't watching—though they were—Rosy scooted under the window sash, picked her way carefully through a hole in the screen, and flew right into the middle of White Rose Cottage.

ten

osy didn't know where to start, Louisa's room was such a shambles. But she remembered what Clara always told the sisters when they had a hard task ahead: Don't take it on all at once. Do one small job at a time, and soon your work will be done.

So Rosy began. She untangled the yarn and cast on twenty stitches. She tidied up the pickup sticks and counted all the playing cards (two decks, forty-nine cards each). She threaded needles, wound up bobbins, and organized all the snippets of fabric into piles by color. She set the painting out to dry, then she sorted the

potholder loops (and started a very pretty potholder). Finally, she made a quick trip out to the
garden to pick some wildflowers, which she
placed in a jam jar. Then she hovered over the

dresser and allowed a small slice of sunlight to warm her wings. She felt very pleased indeed.

"Now when Louisa wakes up, she won't feel so dismal," she said in a whisper. "And no one will ever know it was a fairy's handiwork."

But something wasn't quite right. Rosy squinted at the room to see what was out of place. Nothing was, though it was hard to be sure in the dim light. That's when Rosy realized what was wrong.

"I'll just open the shutters a tiny bit so Louisa can get some light. And air." She flew over to the shutters on the French doors and tried to heave them open. It wasn't easy. They were heavy. And stiff with disuse.

She tugged.

And pulled.

And with a loud *SQUWARRK* . . .

. . . the shutters flew open and light flooded the room.

Louisa jumped up in bed, her eyes open wide. Rosy kept perfectly still. She didn't dare move a wingtip. Louisa lay back down and closed her eyes. Rosy quickly flew toward the window. *Don't see me, don't see me*, she willed.

Just as she lit on the windowsill, a voice broke the silence. Rosy froze.

"You're too big for a bee and too still for a hummingbird. . . ."

Louisa's voice was full of wonder. Rosy was barely breathing now.

"Could you be . . . a fairy?"

eleven

f I said you could *imagine* how Rosy felt, I'd be fibbing. I don't believe any of us can imagine how Rosy felt, as none of us has been a fairy, much less a fairy caught by a Summer Child. When she remembered to breathe again, Rosy silently inched toward the hole in the screen and hoped Louisa would think it was all a dream.

But she was to have no such luck. Louisa got up from her bed much faster than Rosy thought she'd be able to. She caught Rosy in her hands and cupped them around her. Rosy's heart raced. Would she be crushed by this Summer

Person? Would the big telescope things come and chase all the fairies from their homes? And if they did—would Rosy be to blame? She was trembling like an autumn leaf.

But Louisa's hands were gentle, and her voice soft.

"You *are* a fairy!" whispered Louisa. "You *are* real!"

She can see me, thought Rosy.

"I can see bits of you," said Louisa, as if she were reading Rosy's thoughts. "Oh, you're so lovely! You have red hair! You're wearing a . . . pink skirt, maybe? And your wings! They're amazing! I've never seen anything so beautiful in my whole life. Are you for real?"

Louisa put out her finger and stroked Rosy's wings, very, very gingerly.

"You are the prettiest thing ever!"

Rosy couldn't bear so much attention. "My sister Golden is the real beauty of the family," she said.

"You can talk!" cried Louisa. Rosy could not believe she had opened her mouth. "And you have a sister?"

"I shouldn't even be talking to you, much less telling you about my sisters," said Rosy in a rush.

"Sisters!"

"Now you know there's more than one!" She clapped her hand over her mouth. "You shouldn't even know about me. If Queen Mab found out—"

"Queen Mab?"

"Oh, please let me fly away."

Louisa opened her hands. "I won't keep you here if it's not good for you. You can go, little fairy. I'm just glad I saw you. My grammie always said there were fairies on Sheepskerry Island."

Rosy beat her wings as fast as she could and zoomed over to the windowsill. As she clambered through the screen, she took one more look at Louisa. Louisa gave her a little smile and a wave.

Rosy hesitated for just one moment. "My name is Rosy," she said, before she flew away.

twelve

"Where were you?"

Rosy got back to the Bell sisters' fairy house much later than she'd wanted to.

"We missed you down at Lupine Pond," said Goldie. "I suppose you took off somewhere with your book."

Rosy didn't say a word.

"Are you all right?" asked Sylva. "You seem a bit peaky."

"I'm just tired," said Rosy. For the first time in her life, she did not know what to say to her sisters. Could she mention Louisa? She so hated to keep secrets. "I met the most—"

"You should have seen us down at Lupine Pond!" said Sylva as she threw herself at her big sister. "Poppy and I jumped in from the highest branch. Actually, I jumped from the highest branch and Poppy was going to, but then she hopped down a level and jumped from there. But we made the biggest splash!"

"You almost drenched Iris Flower's wings, which she was none too happy about," said Clara.

"We *had* to jump after Squeakie said, 'Tsk-tsk!' didn't we, Squeakie? You wanted us to do it, so we did it!" And Sylva spun Squeakie around in a circle.

"That's enough of that, Sylva," said Clara. She was fixing a salad to go with their dinner. "Goldie, could you fly out to the garden and see if any tomatoes are ripe?"

"I'm in the middle of rinsing my hair," said

Goldie, who was nowhere near the outdoor fairy shower. "Rosy's not busy, are you, Rosy?"

"No, I'm not busy." Rosy was relieved to get out of the house.

As she flitted into the garden, she thought hard about what she had done that day. Something that had started as an act of kindness was now turning into a secret she was keeping from her sisters. She picked off a few cherry tomatoes from the vine. They were still green, and she didn't even notice.

"If I don't tell the others," she said to the blue heron in the pond at the end of their garden, "I'll be keeping something from them. And I've never done that before."

The heron bent a knee, backward.

"But if I do tell them," she said, "they'll have to tell Queen Mab. And she'll—"

"Rosy!"

It couldn't be.

"Rosy!"

Rosy froze. That wasn't Clara's voice or Goldie's or Sylva's. That was Louisa!

"Quiet! Oh, please be quiet!" cried Rosy. She shot up above the hedge around their fairy house so she could see where Louisa was and stop her from calling out again. What if her sisters heard?

"What are you doing up here in Cathedral Pines?" asked Rosy. "It's such a long walk from your cottage. Especially on crutches!"

"These crutches aren't so bad. And I just had to see you again," said Louisa, "to know it wasn't a dream. Grammie told me the fairies lived up here. She said I would see a fairy one day."

"But now everyone will know about us, and they'll run us out of our houses and—"

"No, no! I won't do that. I would never do that. I won't tell a soul, I promise. I'll only tell Grammie when I talk to her on the phone. She already knows you live here! She told me so many stories about the fairies, and I knew they were true. She said she once met Tinker Bell herself!"

"Rosy!" A clear voice rang out. It was Clara.

"Your grandmother met Tink?"

"Tinker Bell. Yes, that's what she said. Grammie gave her something precious, but I can't remember what it was."

"A pink shell! She gave Tink a pink shell! I know all about it!"

"Rosy!" Clara's voice was louder.

"You do?"

"Yes! Yes. I'll tell you more tomorrow." Rosy had to find out more about Louisa's grammie and Tinker Bell.

"Come up to White Rose Cottage," said Louisa. "I'll wait for you there!"

"I'll see you there—at noon!" said Rosy. "Be careful on the boardwalk, Lulu—it's slippery."

Rosy watched for a moment as Louisa turned back toward the cottage. Her pace was strong and even.

"Coming, Clara!" And off she flew.

"What took you so long?" asked Sylva when Rosy flew in the back door.

"And where are the tomatoes?" Goldie asked.

Rosy couldn't trust herself to say a word.

"I think I'd better go to bed. I don't feel too well."

Rosy flitted toward the stairs. She had to bite her tongue to keep from talking.

"Ro-Ro?" said Squeak.

"Oh, I'm so sorry, Squeakie!" Rosy was

shocked at herself. "I didn't even say good night to you." She gave Squeak a fierce hug, and flew upstairs.

"Rosy? Are you quite all right?" asked Clara.

"I'm fine. I'm fine. I'll be fine," she called. "Don't worry."

Clara hadn't been worrying. Until then.

An uneasy silence fell over the sisters.

"Rosy didn't seem herself at all," said Clara at last. "And now she's not even going to have supper."

"She probably had too much activity today," said Goldie.

"But she spent the whole day reading," said Sylva.

"I'm sure there's nothing wrong," said Clara. But she decided to keep an eye on Rosy, just in case.

thirteen

"**S**hall I show you the attic, Rosy?" asked Louisa the next day. "That's where Grammie keeps all her treasures."

"How will you get to the attic with your leg the way it is?" asked Rosy.

"I think I'm strong enough to climb the stairs," said Louisa.

Attic stairs are as quirky as attics themselves. Some are ordinary—a staircase from the top floor. Some are narrow and dark. Some twist. And some come down from a trapdoor like a ladder.

The steps to the attic in White Rose Cottage

were in a far back bedroom, but they were the ordinary sort, which was lucky for Louisa. She had to clomp up each one with her crutches, but she was soon at the top. Rosy rode up on her shoulder and relaxed just a little. She loved attics: their slanted light, their musty, long-ago smells.

Getting away from her sisters that morning had been easier than Rosy thought it would be. Sylva had come running into her room to wake her up, and Rosy had told her she was sleeping in today.

"You never sleep in!" Sylva had said.

"Almost never," Rosy had replied.

"But we're going fishing in Nettle Pond."

"You go ahead, and I'll meet up with you later. Catch some minnows for me!"

Rosy sighed, remembering what she'd said to Sylva. It wasn't quite a lie. But it wasn't quite true, either.

"Look, Rosy!" called Louisa. She was in a

small sunlit corner of the attic, sitting on an old step stool on the floor. "This is what I was looking for!"

Rosy flew over and found the perfect perch on a paraffin lantern on top of a dusty side table. Louisa had pulled out a book.

"Here it is," she said. "This is the book about Tinker Bell."

Rosy took in a quick breath. Right there before her eyes was a book—an old, crumbling book—about her very own big sister.

You might be wondering why there was such an old book about Tink when she has such young sisters. Some of you already know that fairy years are very different from our years—sometimes longer, sometimes shorter. Tink had managed to stay the same age for a very long time.

"I think that when my grammie was a little girl, Tink was little, too," said Louisa. "That's before she got to be so famous."

"Your grammie was famous?"

"No, silly! Tinker Bell is famous. Listen to this!"

Louisa flipped the pages of the book till she came to the place she was looking for. "It's a story about Tink and Peter Pan," she said.

Rosy knew Tink lived on a faraway island called Neverland with Peter Pan, but she didn't know much more than that. The Fairy Bell sisters, in truth, rarely heard from Tink these days. Except for the occasional postcard, written on birch bark and delivered by a team of swallows, they had no real idea what Tink was up to.

"Let me read you this part," said Louisa. "Peter is talking to Wendy about your sister Tinker Bell."

"Who's Wendy?" asked Rosy. Tinker Bell had never mentioned anyone by that name.

"Wendy's a real girl like me!"

Rosy fluttered her wings. Did Tink have a secret friend, too?

"Listen," Louisa said. Then she started to read:

"Wendy," Peter whispered gleefully, "I do believe I shut her up in the drawer!"

"Peter Pan shut my big sister up in a drawer?" said Rosy. "Tink would not like that at all."

"It's not for long," said Louisa. "I'll read you the next part."

He let poor Tink out of the drawer, and she flew about the nursery screaming with fury.

"That sounds like Tink," said Rosy.

Louisa kept reading:

"O Peter," cried Wendy, "if she would only stand still and let me see her!"

Louisa looked up at Rosy. "Do you suppose that's how I came to see you in my room yesterday? Because you were so very still?"

"I think it must have been," said Rosy. "But never mind me. What happens next?"

fourteen

Every day after that, Rosy escaped from Cathedral Pines for a few minutes here and there to meet Louisa at White Rose Cottage to hear the story of Peter Pan and Wendy and Tink and the Lost Boys and Captain Hook.

"Let's meet every day—" said Louisa.

"At noon—"

"And if we can't meet up one day, let's leave each other a secret message," said Louisa.

"Oh yes! We'll have a little post office of our own," said Rosy.

They found an old biscuit tin with a tight lid that became their secret post office.

"I'll put it on the corner of the sleeping porch on the second floor," said Louisa.

"Isn't that too far for you?"

"No! These crutches are great," Louisa exclaimed. And indeed by now she was getting along very well with them. "No one will find it there."

Every day, as the long days of August stretched before them, they met in secret. Rosy told Louisa all about the Fairy Bell sisters— how Clara was so wise, and Golden so clever. She even told Louisa about the time Sylva came to the Fairy Ball.

"You are so lucky," Louisa told Rosy. "I wish I had sisters like you do."

One day, when it was rainy, they took shelter in the playhouse in the back of the cottage garden. "Grammie always called this a Wendy house," said Louisa. "She named it after Wendy in the book."

Rosy looked around the comfy playhouse. "That must have made Tink pretty jealous!" she said.

"Are any of your sisters like her? Not Goldie or Clara, and not you. Or Sylva, I guess. Maybe Baby Squirt?"

Rosy laughed. "It's Squeak!" she said. "And her real name is Euphemia."

"Euphemia!" said Louisa. "What a big name for a little fairy!"

"I think she will grow into it," said Rosy.

Louisa asked all sorts of questions then. How many fairies lived on Sheepskerry (lots), and did fairies live anywhere else in the world (yes), and could Louisa meet them?

"I'm not sure . . . ," said Rosy.

"But why not?" asked Louisa. "Why can't Summer People and fairies be friends? We're doing okay, aren't we?"

Rosy thought about the fairies of Coombe Meadow. She thought about what her sisters would say if they knew about Louisa.

"It's still too dangerous, Lulu," said Rosy. "I don't know if I can ever introduce you to the other fairies. Or my sisters."

Louisa did not say anything for a while. At last she turned to Rosy. "I guess you just want me to read some more," she said. "And my name is actually Louisa."

The rest of that day did not go so well.

Louisa read the story, but Rosy hardly heard a word. Rosy was keeping Lulu away from her sisters, and keeping her sisters away from Lulu. Her head was pounding by the end of the day, when she flew into the fairy house just before everyone else arrived.

"Another headache?" asked Clara.

"A doozy," said Rosy. She kissed her big sister absently on the cheek and flitted upstairs to bed.

fifteen

Rosy wanted to say sorry to Louisa the next day, but she wasn't sure that Louisa would want to see her. The air was still; the birds weren't chirping and the brown squirrels were quiet. Rosy could sense in her wingtips that a storm was on the way—a powerful storm, out of the northeast. With the weather threatening, Rosy felt it was even more important to get a message to Lulu. She sat at the small writing desk in her room and wrote a note with blackberry ink:

Dear Louisa,
I cannot come to see you today.
I will come tomorrow.

She considered for a minute before she ended
her letter. Then she added,

I'd like you to meet my sisters, too.
                                    Love,
                                    Rosy

Rosy took the note and tucked it under her
arm. She started out to the secret post office
box. "Are you putting it in the snail mailbox?"
asked Clara. "I'm heading that way myself. I can
take it for you so we aren't both caught in the
rain."

"Oh no," Rosy replied. "I'll be happy to take
it on my own. I'm just going to do a quick lap

around the Pines. I need to get some air before we're cooped up in here by the storm."

Clara let Rosy leave first. Then she followed her.

Rosy was almost out of sight in the moment it took Clara to follow her out the door, and she was definitely not going for a lap around the Pines. Rosy was heading down the path toward Sea Glass Beach.

Clara was so relieved she caught an updraft and flew high into the air.

"Oh, that's what Rosy's doing!" She fluttered her wings. "She's collecting blue sea glass for Golden. Typical of her—even if it's a bit chancy. Rosy!" called Clara. "I'll help you!" And she darted down to Sea Glass Beach.

She saw one of the Summer Children down on the beach—a bit too far out on the rocks, she thought. But Rosy was not there.

Clara flew upward again. She steadied herself against the wind.

No Rosy on Sea Glass Beach. No Rosy heading to Seal Rock. No Rosy on her way to Lady's Slipper Field. And certainly no Rosy anywhere near White Rose—

Clara's wings skipped a beat. It couldn't be! But it was. Rosy was winging her way up to the sleeping porch of a Summer Family's cottage.

"What is she doing?" cried Clara. Her head was ringing with alarm. "She's getting way too close!"

With a galloping heart, Clara followed her sister to the sleeping porch. She saw Rosy open up a small tin box and take out a note. Clara's eyes were sharp. The note was on yellow paper . . . with lines. And it was written in pencil, not in blackberry ink. That meant the

note could not have been written by a fairy.

It could only have been written by a Summer Child.

Clara reeled back in amazement and fear. Had her own sister betrayed the fairy code?

Sixteen

"Rosy! ROSY!" Clara shouted.

Rosy looked around in alarm. "Clara! What are you doing here? Get away from the cottage."

Rosy was caught! And that wasn't even the worst of it. She had read Louisa's note. And this is what it said:

Dear Rosy,

In case you come today (which you probably won't) you won't find me here. I have gone down to Sea Glass Beach to find some blue sea glass for Goldie.

Your friend even if you don't think so,

Lulu

Rosy looked up at the sky. It had a dark, coppery cast to it. The air was chilly now, and raw. The wind was rustling the trees so much that all Rosy could see were the undersides of their leaves.

"Rosy Harmonia Bell! Come with me at once!"

"Clara! I can't go home with you. If Louisa's on Sea Glass Beach in this storm, she might never come back!"

Rosy flew as fast as her wings could carry her down to Sea Glass Beach. Clara was right behind her, but Rosy couldn't talk now. She just had to find Louisa.

Hovering high in the air, Rosy could see the whole beach. There was Louisa, on the rocks. And one of her crutches had fallen onto the beach below.

"Rosy—listen to me. Listen to me!" cried Clara. "We have to go, at once!"

"But she's lost a crutch," said Rosy. "And if we don't help her get it back, she'll be stuck here. Terrible things could happen."

"Rosy, it's too bad! Someone else will come get her. She's not your concern. The welfare of the fairies is what comes first, not this Summer Child."

"She's not just a Summer Child. She's my friend," cried Rosy. She swooped down to be next to Louisa, leaving Clara hovering in the air.

"Oh, Rosy," said Louisa. "I'm so sorry about yesterday."

"No, *I'm* sorry!" said Rosy. "Of course you should meet my sisters. You should meet all the fairies. But first we have to get you out of here."

"Rosy! Leave her and come home!" Clara called.

"Go, Rosy," said Louisa. "Go now before they send you away from Sheepskerry Island. I'll be okay. I'm sure of it."

"Rosy! Now!"

With heavy tears in her eyes, Rosy turned and left Louisa. She followed Clara home.

Seventeen

"**Y**ou are a disgrace," said Clara as they swiftly flew toward Cathedral Pines. It was the worst thing she had ever said to her sister. "I'm ashamed of you. You've betrayed us all. I'm only glad that no one else knows your secret."

Rosy scarcely heard her. What if no one realized Louisa was missing, or just thought she was safely curled up in her room with a book? "I'm proud that Lulu is my friend!" she cried.

"No Summer Child can be your friend!" said Clara.

"That's not true!" said Rosy. "Tinker Bell

was a good friend to a Summer Child. Lulu's own grammie gave Tink the pink shell on our mantel, Clara. There was a time when children played with fairies, and fairies were their friends. It can be like that again."

"No, it can't!" cried Clara. "That time has gone!"

"You're wrong, Clara. You're wrong!" Rosy's voice was hoarse and choked. "I'm going back."

"Rosy, no!"

But Rosy had already flown off, into the teeth of the storm.

Louisa was not where Rosy had left her. She looked out into the bay, but all she could see were the tails of the mermaids as they played in the wild waves. The mermaids loved storms, for storms brought treasure.

"Lulu! Lulu!" called Rosy. "Lulu, where are you?"

She heard a faint voice. "Rosy! You came back!"

Louisa had taken shelter behind a huge rock. "I'm trying to get my crutch," she said. "It's down on the beach."

"Don't go out any farther!" called Rosy. "I'll get it for you." Rosy didn't know how she could do it, though. The crutch was too heavy. And the tide was higher than she'd ever seen it.

"Let me see if I can drag it up," said Rosy, as the first hard raindrops began to fall.

Rosy heaved and hauled, but she could not get the crutch to budge. "I need help, and I'm not going to get any. There's only one thing for it—I'll have to fly back to your cottage and show myself to your parents."

"But they don't believe in fairies. Your voice will just sound like a wind chime to them."

"I'll make them understand! I'll make them understand somehow!" Rosy was crying now. How had things gotten into such a terrible mess? She flew down close to Louisa. "I don't know what will happen, Lulu. But I'm so glad you are my secret friend."

"Me too," whispered Louisa. "Me too."

Just then they heard a sound they could scarcely believe. The sound of beating wings. Many, many beating wings. It couldn't be the birds—they were hiding from the storm. It couldn't be the bees—they were safely in their hive. That meant it could only be—

"Clara! Goldie! Sylva! You've come to save us!"

"Not just us, Rosy!"

Behind the Bell sisters came an army of fairies. Iris, Susan, and Poppy Flower, the Bakewells, the Blossoms, all the Cobwebs, and the Jellicoes, even Julia. "Where's Squeakie?" cried Rosy.

"She's safe with Daisy Flower," said Clara.

"All these fairies have come to help . . . me?" asked Louisa.

"Yes, and we must make quick work of it," said Clara. "If we all pull together, we'll get you back to the cottage before the storm gets worse. Come on, fairies!"

Like a swarm, the fairies flew down to the beach and landed on Louisa's crutch. Sylva and Poppy were holding hands.

"Now, lift! Together!" cried Clara. And together, they heaved up Louisa's crutch, just moments before it was swept out to sea.

"Heigh-ho!" sang the mermaids. "A few more laps of the waves and it would have been ours,"

they wailed. "We had plans for that crutch. We were going to use it to bargain with a pirate for gold doubloons." Then they flipped back into the roiling sea.

The fairies flew Louisa's crutch back up to her as the rain came down in sheets. It was very hard work. Rain slows a fairy down like nothing else on earth. "Let me help you, fairies. Perch in my pockets and I'll get you to shelter."

The fairies, nervous as they were, knew they had best do as she said.

"We'll take refuge in your cottage till the worst of the storm is over," said Clara. "It's the only thing we can do now."

There's an expression from the old days, "Safe as houses," but houses don't feel so safe in a storm such as this. The trees all but break their backs in the wind. The sea rages and roils. The rain pelts down on the roofs and drowns out every thought. Branches break. Forgotten deck chairs topple over and blow across the lawns.

"Almost there," said Goldie, who had taken a place in Louisa's front pocket. "I, for one, will be happy when this is over."

Louisa stopped on the porch of White Rose Cottage.

"Is that you, Lulu?" called her mother. "I know you're doing great with your crutches, but don't go out in this storm."

"Oh, I won't, Mom," said Louisa. She could feel the fairies shivering in her pockets, and she knew it wasn't from cold.

"It's all right, sweet fairies," she said. "No harm will come to you here."

The fairies huddled together in the tiny storeroom next to the White Rose playroom. They toweled off with washcloths provided by Louisa, and blew on one another's wings till they were perfectly dry. The storm raged for hours. Only the sound of Louisa's sure voice reading the story of Tinker Bell and Peter Pan got them through it.

At last, as the day ended, the setting sun broke through the clouds. The sea sparkled, and the whole island was as green as an emerald. The day, which had started so tumultuously, ended in peace.

"Fairies, all," said Clara. "The storm has passed. Time to fly back home."

eighteen

"Our fairy houses," said Blanche Cobweb. "They're gone."

Cathedral Pines was in ruins, but the houses weren't quite gone, as Blanche at first thought. In a way, what was left was worse. The Bell sisters' roof was on top of the Flower sisters' chimney. The Bakewell sisters' ovens were a heap of rubble. The Jellicoes' jars of jam were smashed against the rocks. And the few precious items that did remain were smeared in mud.

"It will take a long time—all the way till winter—to rebuild," said Clara as she picked up debris, "but we will get it done."

"I wish we had a little bit of magic to help us," said Goldie.

"Queen Mab will help," said Sylva. "Just as soon as she hears what happened."

"Do you think Tink would come and bring her magic if we got a message to her?"

"Maybe," said Clara. But after hearing the story Louisa read, she was less certain than ever that Tink would come home.

"I suppose we'll have to start now."

And so the fairies got to work. They heaved branches and dragged leaves. They gathered moss for their lawns and stones for their paths. The younger fairies collected crockery and cutlery that had been swept up by the storm.

Suddenly they heard a trampling through

the woods. It got louder and louder.

"It's the Summer People!"

"You said Louisa wouldn't tell!"

"She promised! She promised she wouldn't say anything to anyone."

"Run, fairies, run for your lives!"

But just as the fairies were about to fly away, Louisa's voice rang out.

"Rosy? Rosy! I've brought the other children. To help."

Through the wet branches emerged the Summer Children. They were all there: six cottages, eighteen children. All looking around eagerly. All very quiet and respectful. All wanting to help.

"Rosy, you saved my life, so now we can save your houses. We can help you if you'll let us."

"Do you think we should let them?" asked Sylva.

The children waited, still as statues.

"I'm just not sure," said Clara. "There are so many of them."

"What if they—"

"Tsk-tsk!" said Squeak.

"What did you say, Squeakie?" said Rosy.

"Tsk-TSK!" cried Squeak.

Rosy looked at Clara. Clara smiled.

"You're right, Squeakie!" Clara said. "Let's do it!"

At first the children were not very good at fairy-house building. They had never done it before, and they didn't know how. A few of them recalled their grandparents (and a few parents) trying to teach them many long years ago, but since they hadn't believed in fairies at the time, they remembered nothing.

The Cobwebs and the Blossoms were shy around the Summer Children, but Golden Bell certainly had no trouble bossing them about.

"Birch bark for the walls, you ninnies, not flaky sycamore," she said. "Fetch some moss for our floors, please, and you boys, come move the stones into place in the garden."

As a result of Goldie's confident direction, the Bell house was finished first. "Pah-pah!" cried Squeakie as she and her sisters flew back into their house, now sturdy and strong.

"I am so happy to be snug at home," said Sylva. "I think I'll go see what Poppy's house looks like." And she flew out the door.

Clara was just glad to have everything set to rights. Goldie was checking her wardrobe and her dressmaking supplies—all there. Rosy was watching with joy as the children

helped the other fairies put their houses back together.

"It seems the Summer Children are different than we thought they were," said Clara as dusk fell.

"I'm sorry I kept such a big secret from you, Clara."

"I'm sorry I didn't listen to what you were trying to tell me," said Clara. "They did believe in fairies after all. I hope we'll meet more children like that someday."

nineteen

August, which usually dragged by so slowly, hastened to its end. After the storm, the weather was crystal clear, and on Leaving Day the sky was a heartbreaking blue.

Louisa couldn't quite run down the boardwalk to the dock, but she moved so fast it was hard to believe she still had a cast on her foot. "You're so much better!" cried Rosy.

"I know! And I get this dumb cast off as soon as we get home!" She was smiling broadly. "It's all thanks to you and your kindness," she added. "Now I have a wonderful new friend on Sheepskerry Island."

"I wonder if you will be able to see us again next year, when you come back," said Sylva. For all her boldness, she was still a little wary of Louisa and the Summer Children.

"Why wouldn't I?" asked Louisa.

"Sometimes children grow too old to believe in fairies," said Goldie. "They think the beating of our wings is just sunlight glinting. They think the music of our voices is just wind chimes blowing. Maybe it won't happen next year, but—"

"It never happened to my grammie, and it will never happen to me," said Louisa.

Clara just smiled.

"Here, I want you to have this." Rosy had rescued Tink's pink shell from the wreckage of the storm. "Your grammie gave this to our family. Now we're giving it back to you. As a thank-you for rebuilding our houses."

"And bringing back the trust between the fairies and the Summer Children."

"Next year, we won't need to have secrets from each other."

The fairies lined up on the white railings down by the dock and waved good-bye to the Summer Children. The Summer Children waved back. Their parents just batted at their

hair and ears, as if mosquitoes were buzzing.

The ferry driver started the motor, and the ferry, low in the water with its cargo of Summer People, pulled out from the dock.

"Good-bye, Rosy!" called Louisa.

"Don't you mean, good-bye White Rosy Cottage?" asked her mother.

Louisa grinned.

"Bye-bye, Lulu!" called Rosy. "See you next year, I hope!"

Clara, Golden, and Sylva waved till the ferry was just a speck on the diamond waves of the bay. Clara looked around and allowed herself a contented smile.

"Sometimes I wonder what it would be like to live on the mainland," said Golden.

"Not me," said Sylva. "I think it's terrific to have the island to ourselves again. I can't wait till Queen Mab comes back so we can tell her all about our adventure."

"Somehow," said Clara, "I think she'll already know."

The Fairy Bell sisters stretched their wings and turned to leave. "Coming, Rosy?"

Rosy was still watching the open water, though the ferry had all but disappeared. "I'll just stay a bit longer," said Rosy. "You go home. I'll be there soon."

Rosy strained her eyes as she looked toward the horizon.

"Good-bye, my secret friend," said Rosy quietly as the boat disappeared from view. "I wonder what next summer will bring."

fairy secrets

Squeak's Words

Hmm: The beach

Wuh?: Can't you do something?

Dhaah: Dark

Tsk-tsk!: Do it!

Lay-lay-lay: They're coming

Pah-pah: Amazing

Odeo: Oh, dear

Ro-Ro: Rosy

Squeak!: Oops! or Uh-oh!
or Yay! or sometimes, *Yikes!*

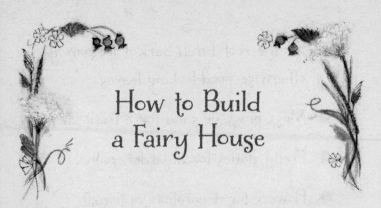

How to Build a Fairy House

It takes ages and ages for fairies to build their own houses, so oh, how they love it when someone else does all the hard work for them! I'm told that if a child builds a fairy house with thoughtfulness and care, even if it's in a busy city park or a sleepy backyard, fairies might be bold enough to move right in and stay for a good long time.

What you'll need to build a fairy house:

* Some twigs for the walls

* Acorns, chestnuts, shells, or other smooth objects for chairs and tables

❋ For the roof: birch bark if it's handy; otherwise, good-looking leaves

❋ Moss, grass, or sand for a front lawn

❋ Pretty stones for a garden path

❋ Flowers for decoration (optional)

Find a spot that fairies would like. (Usually, it's the kind of spot that you would like.)

Place the twigs into the ground in the shape of a house: either a square or a circle or a triangle or a rectangle, or something in between.

Add furniture in whatever way you think would be most comfortable for fairies.

Carefully lay the birch bark or leaves on top for a roof.

Spread grass or moss or sand in front of the house for a lawn. Make a backyard, too, if you have enough space.

Put the pretty stones in a line or a double line for a garden path. The path can be straight or it can weave around.

Decorate with flowers, as many as you like.

Send good thoughts out to the world, go to bed, and in the morning—if luck is with you—you'll see signs that the fairies have come.

A word to the wise: This may turn into quite a project, as once you build one fairy house, you might have to build a few more. Fairies are very neighborly and like to have lots of friends and family nearby.

The Song of Sheepskerry Island

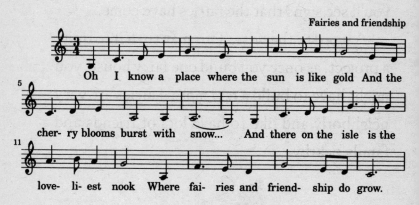

Fairies and friendship

Oh I know a place where the sun is like gold And the cher- ry blooms burst with snow... And there on the isle is the love- li- est nook Where fai- ries and friend- ship do grow.

An excerpt from

Golden
at the
Fancy-Dress Party

The Fairy Bell Sisters

Book 3

Queen Mab smiled. "My beloved fairy family," she said. "Some exciting news! I've had word from my cousin on the mainland, Queen Titania."

"I hope it's not bad news," whispered Clara.

Goldie's wings quivered again. "I don't think so," she said.

"To celebrate the season and to bring joy to the long autumn nights, Queen Titania is hosting a fancy-dress party on the mainland."

"The mainland?" said Goldie. Her heart skipped a beat. She had never been to the mainland. None of the Bell sisters ever had—except Tinker Bell, of course. It was three days' flight from Sheepskerry, too long and too dangerous a journey for young fairies. Goldie kept her wings as still as she could. A fancy-dress party on the mainland? Why, she would give her *wings* to attend!

"A fancy-dress party," whispered Poppy Flower to her best friend, Sylva. "What's that?"

"It's a dress-up party," said Sylva. "Where you wear costumes."

"Ooh!" said Poppy. "I love to dress up!"

Goldie did not say a word. She was the best at dress-up on the whole island. Everyone knew that.

"Just one fairy from each island may attend the fancy-dress party," said Queen Mab. Then she peered out and looked right at the Fairy Bell sisters. Quietly, she said to them, "Queen Titania hasn't yet learned the lesson you taught us, Sylva, at the Fairy Ball."

Sylva blushed.

Queen Mab's voice grew loud again. "There will be a prize for the best costume in Fairyland. And Queen Titania has asked us to send one fairy from Sheepskerry to take part."

"Ooh, Goldie," said Rosy. "No wonder your wings were quivering. You should go."

Goldie held her breath.

"I'd like you all to think who would create a costume that will make Sheepskerry proud," said Queen Mab. "I would rather show pride in our fairy island than win, as I'm sure you know."

Fern Stitch flew straight up to Queen Mab. The Fairy Bell sisters could not hear what she was saying, but later they heard about the conversation from Iris Flower, who heard it from Sugar Bakewell. "It's true we are known far and wide for our tiny stitching and intricate patterns," Fern had told the queen. "But all three of us think someone else should go to the mainland. Someone else who will make the best costume in the land."

As soon as Fern stepped away from Queen Mab, there was a murmuring in the crowd, as if all the fairies were speaking with one voice. At first it sounded like they were saying, "*Go! Go!*" But then Clara and Rosy and Sylva—and, of course, Goldie—heard more clearly what their fairy friends were saying.

"*Gold-ie! Gold-ie!*" came the cheer.

"Listen!" said Clara.

"I'm listening!" cried Goldie.

"GOLD-IE! GOLD-IE! GOLD-IE!"

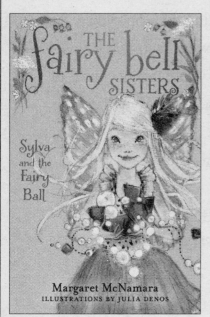